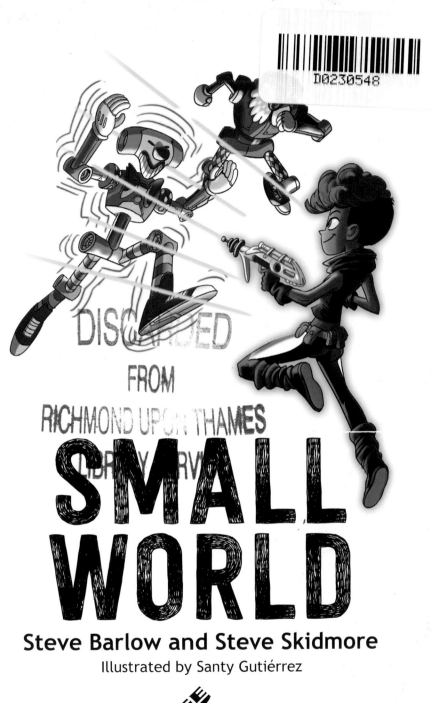

SMALL WORLD

Steve Barlow and Steve Skidmore

Illustrated by Santy Gutiérrez

EDGE FRANKLIN WATTS

LONDON·SYDNEY

Franklin Watts
First published in Great Britain in 2019 by The Watts Publishing Group

Credits
Series Editor: Adrian Cole
Project Editor: Katie Woolley
Consultant: Jackie Hamley
Design Manager: Peter Scoulding
Cover Designer: Cathryn Gilbert
Illustrations: Santiago Gutiérrez

HB ISBN 978 1 4451 5972 0
PB ISBN 978 1 4451 5971 3
Library ebook ISBN 978 1 4451 5970 6

Printed in China.

Franklin Watts
An imprint of
Hachette Children's Group
Part of The Watts Publishing Group
Carmelite House
50 Victoria Embankment
London EC4Y 0DZ

An Hachette UK Company
www.hachette.co.uk

www.franklinwatts.co.uk

THE BADDIES

Lord and
Lady Evil

Dr Y

They want to rule the galaxy.

THE GOODIES

Boo Hoo   Jet   Tip

They want to stop them.

11

13

There was a roar of engines.

Everyone looked up.

"Here come the baddies!" said Boo Hoo.

16

One of the Wees shook his head.

"Why did Lord Evil send *clowns*?"

"I think he meant to send *clones*,"

said Jet.

Dr Y's ray gun shrank the Wees.

"We've got to stop him," said Boo Hoo.

"Cover me!" shouted Jet.

She started to sneak behind Dr Y.

Easy!" said Boo Hoo. "Just like this!"

He pushed Tip.

24

Jet shook Dr Y's gun. "Oh no!
It's jammed..."